GECKO PRESS

Line Up, Please!

Tomoko Ohmura

What's everyone waiting for? Let's go and see...

"This is exciting!"

"It sure is!"

"One, two. One, two."

"Wow! What a long queue!"

"It's always like this."

Everyone stay in line till we're ready to start!

"So, what are we lining up for?"

"What? You don't know?"

"Pee-yew! What a smell!"

"Whoops... sorry."

Weasel
42

Hedgehog
41

Rabbit
40

Armadillo
39

Skunk
38

Porcupine
37

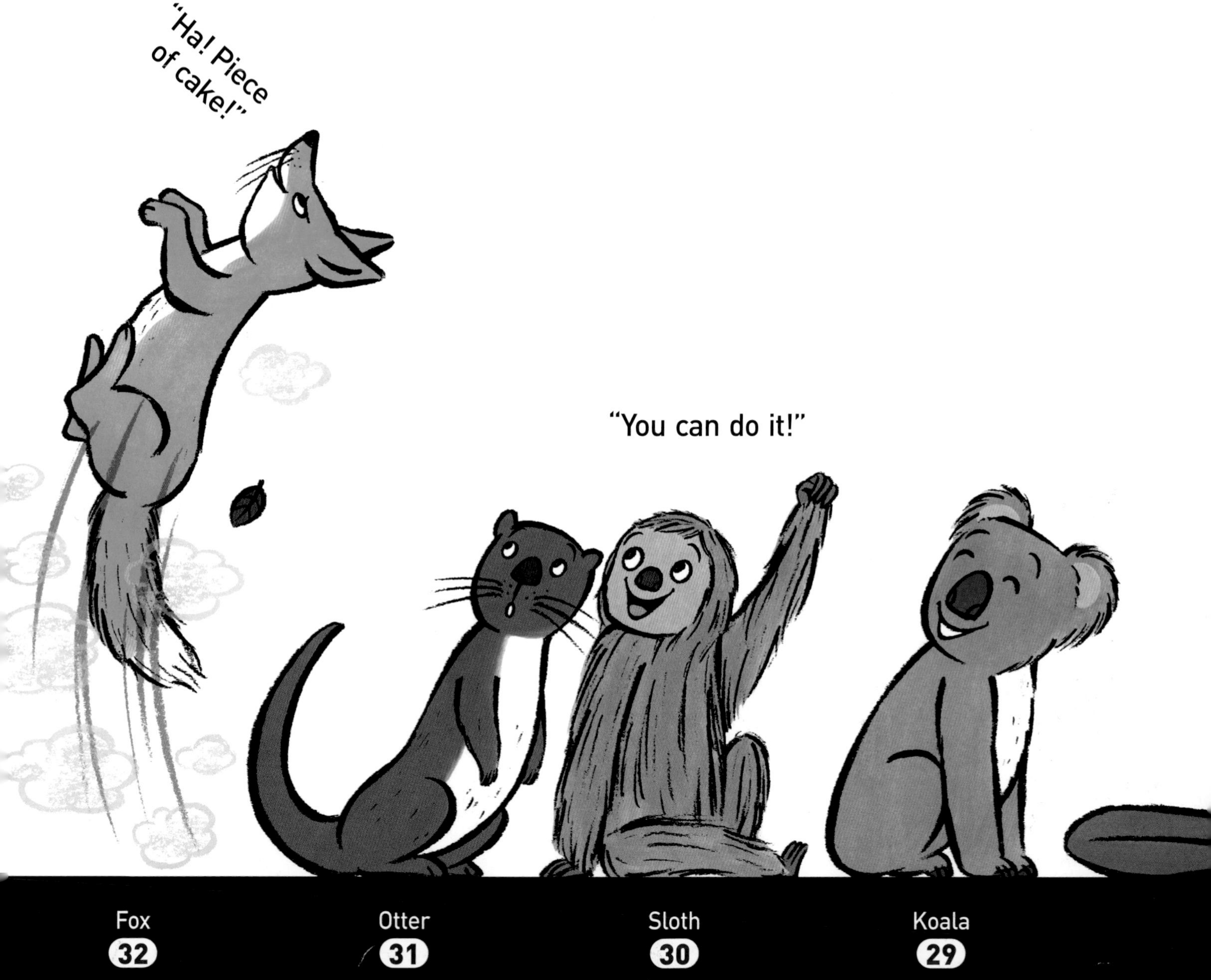
"Ha! Piece of cake!"
"You can do it!"
Fox
32
Otter
31
Sloth
30
Koala
29

"Can I have a bit more room?"

"There's a gap up there."

"You're too close."

"I can't help it."

Beaver
28

Chimpanzee
27

Orangutan
26

Goat
25

Pig
24

"But I'm scared..."

"Let's play
Word Chain."

All right.
Let me see...
Bird!

"That's a D...deer!"

Panda
17

Cow
16

"R...rabbit."

"T...turtle."

"E...ewe?"

"Eagle."

"I want some, too."

Tiger

7

"Yaaaawwwn.
How much longer?"

Any minute now!

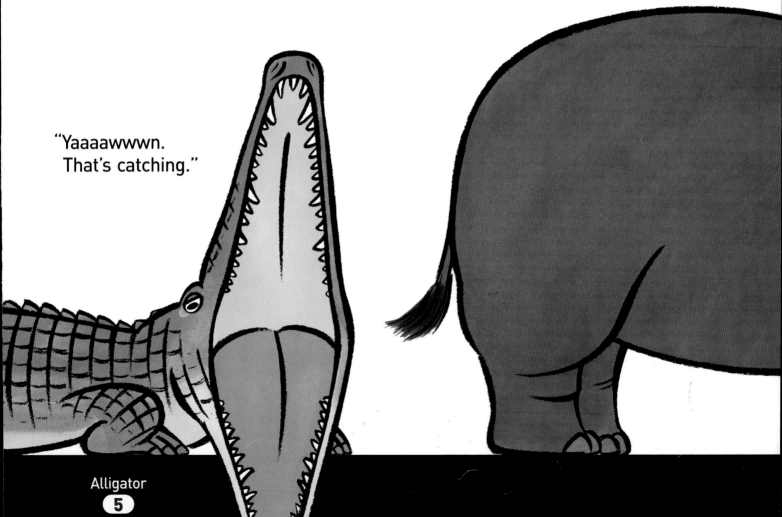

"Yaaaawwwn.
That's catching."

Alligator
5

"I can't wait
another second!"

"I'm going to charge."

YIPPEE

Here we go!

Two!

Three!

SWOOOSSS

WE MADE

"That was worth waiting for."

"I don't want to get off."

"That was fun!"

That was fun! Shall we go again?

TODAY'S GUEST LIST

1	Elephant	26	Orangutan
2	Giraffe	27	Chimpanzee
3	Rhinoceros	28	Beaver
4	Hippopotamus	29	Koala
5	Alligator	30	Sloth
6	Camel	31	Otter
7	Tiger	32	Fox
8	Zebra	33	Raccoon
9	Lion	34	Dog
10	Bear	35	Monkey
11	Seal	36	Cat
12	Tapir	37	Porcupine
13	Leopard	38	Skunk
14	Gorilla	39	Armadillo
15	Deer	40	Rabbit
16	Cow	41	Hedgehog
17	Panda	42	Weasel
18	Hyena	43	Guinea Pig
19	Kangaroo	44	Turtle
20	Boar	45	Squirrel
21	Wombat	46	Flying Squirrel
22	Wolf	47	Mole
23	Sheep	48	Mouse
24	Pig	49	Gecko
25	Goat	50	Frog

Ride: Whale
Guide: Bird

For more curiously good books,
visit www.geckopress.com

This edition first published in 2014 by Gecko Press
PO Box 9335, Marion Square, Wellington 6141, New Zealand
info@geckopress.com

Distributed in New Zealand by Random House NZ,
www.randomhouse.co.nz

Distributed in Australia by Scholastic Australia,
www.scholastic.com.au

Distributed in the UK by Bounce Sales & Marketing,
www.bouncemarketing.co.uk

English language edition © Gecko Press Ltd 2014
Reprinted 2015

Original title: Nanno Gyôretsu
© 2009 by Tomoko Ohmura
First published in Japan in 2009 by POPLAR Publishing Co., Ltd.

English language translation rights arranged with
POPLAR Publishing Co., Ltd. through Japan Foreign-Rights Centre

A catalogue record for this book is available from the
National Library of New Zealand.

Translated by Cathy Hirano
Edited by Penelope Todd
Typeset by Vida & Luke Kelly, New Zealand
Printed in China by Everbest Printing Co. Ltd,
an accredited ISO 14001 & FSC certified printer

ISBN hardback: 978-1-877579-98-1
ISBN paperback: 978-1-877579-99-8